First published in the United States 1982 by
Dial Books for Young Readers
A Division of E. P. Dutton, Inc.
2 Park Avenue
New York, New York 10016
Published in Great Britain by Andersen Press Ltd.
Copyright © 1982 by Fulvio Testa
Printed in Italy
Design by Atha Tehon

Library of Congress Cataloging in Publication Data
Testa, Fulvio.
If you take a pencil.
Summary: A counting book that leads
the reader on a fantasy journey.
[1. Drawing—Fiction. 2. Counting] I. Title.
PZ7.T2875If [E] 82-1505
ISBN 0-8037-4023-9   AACR2

US
10 9 8 7 6 5 4 3 2

The art for each picture consists of an ink
and dye painting, which is camera-separated
and reproduced in full color.

If You Take a Pencil

FULVIO TESTA

Dial Books for Young Readers

E. P. DUTTON, INC. *New York*

If you take a pencil, you can draw two cats.

And if they like each other, there will soon be three.

They will flirt with four birds in a golden cage.

And five fingers can give them freedom.

They will fly into a garden with six orange trees.

DAVIS JOINT UNIFIED SCHOOLS
VALLEY OAK ELEMENTARY

Nearby is a fountain with seven jets of fresh water.

In the fountain are eight red fish with blue tails—

blue like the sea where there is a boat with nine sails.

Ten are the sailors.

Eleven are the small islands around the treasure island.

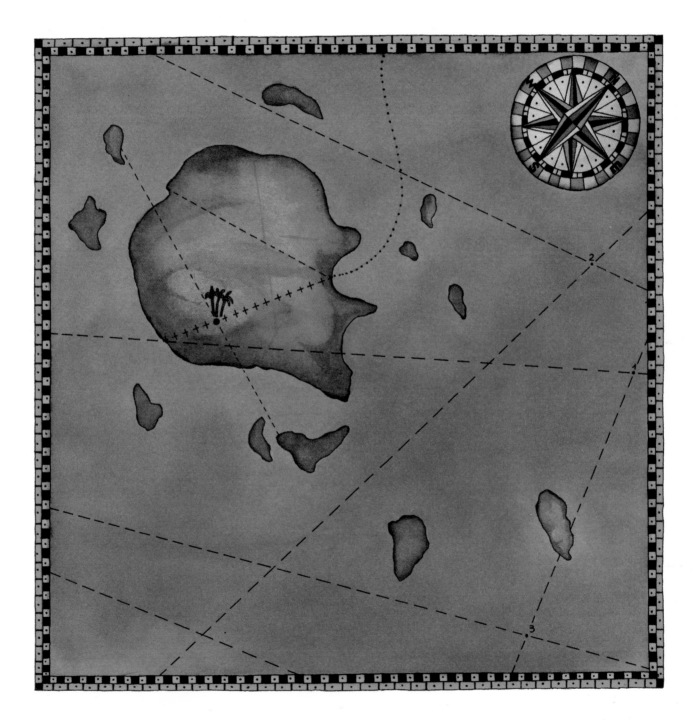

On the island are twelve treasure chests.
They are all empty except one.

You open it. There is a little treasure inside —
a pencil.

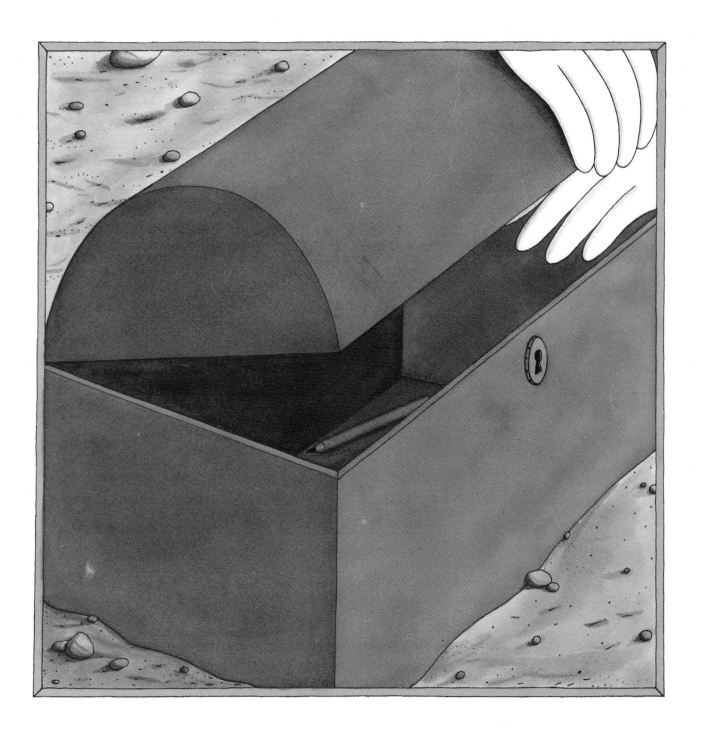